Peanut Butter and Homework Sandwiches

LISA BROADIE COOK · illustrated by JACK E. DAVIS

G. P. PUTNAM'S SONS · AN IMPRINT OF PENGUIN GROUP (USA) INC.

For my mom—
who showed me the joy of books and reading.
—L.B.C.

For Otis—the happiest pup.
He raced through spring. A life filled with great humor and intelligence.
A heart bursting with love. He was our very best friend.
—J.E.D.

G. P. PUTNAM'S SONS

A division of Penguin Young Readers Group. Published by The Penguin Group.
Penguin Group (USA) Inc., 375 Hudson Street, New York, NY 10014, U.S.A.
Penguin Group (Canada), 90 Eglinton Avenue East, Suite 700, Toronto, Ontario M4P 2Y3, Canada (a division of Pearson Penguin Canada Inc.).
Penguin Books Ltd, 80 Strand, London WC2R ORL, England.
Penguin Ireland, 25 St. Stephen's Green, Dublin 2, Ireland (a division of Penguin Books Ltd.).
Penguin Group (Australia), 250 Camberwell Road, Camberwell, Victoria 3124, Australia (a division of Pearson Australia Group Pty Ltd).
Penguin Books India Pvt Ltd, 11 Community Centre, Panchsheel Park, New Delhi - 110 017, India.
Penguin Group (NZ), 67 Apollo Drive, Rosedale, North Shore 0632, New Zealand (a division of Pearson New Zealand Ltd).
Penguin Books (South Africa) (Pty) Ltd, 24 Sturdee Avenue, Rosebank, Johannesburg 2196, South Africa.
Penguin Books Ltd, Registered Offices: 80 Strand, London WC2R ORL, England.

Design by Ryan Thomann. Text set in Chicken Soup.

Library of Congress Cataloging-in-Publication Data is available upon request.
ISBN 978-0-399-24533-6
1 3 5 7 9 10 8 6 4 2

It was Monday, and all Martin MacGregor

wanted to do was go to school. Mr. Elliott was the coolest teacher
ever, and this was the day he was going to bring in his pet—
Harriett the tarantula.

But when Martin burst into class, he was surprised to see a tall lady with orange hair piled on top of her head.

"My name is Mrs. Payne. Mr. Elliott will be out of school for a while."

Martin MacGregor learned two things at school that day. One was Mr. Elliott had broken his arm mountain climbing, and the other was Mrs. Payne loved to give mountains of homework.

After school, Martin MacGregor sat down to do his homework. Just as he worked the last problem, he spied the jar of peanut butter on the kitchen counter.

"Sadie, I need some brain food!" he said.

Martin slopped the peanut butter on one slice of bread
and dripped a mountain of jelly on the other. The peanut butter
and jelly oozed out the side as Martin took a big bite.

Splat! Martin's paper was covered with peanut butter and jelly.

"Oh, great!" Martin got up to get a paper towel. But before he could clean up the mess, Sadie was doing it for him.

"Sadie, you didn't just eat the peanut butter—you ate the whole paper!" yelled Martin. "This gives new meaning to 'the dog ate my homework.' What will Mrs. Payne think?"

On Tuesday morning, when Martin tried to tell Mrs. Payne that his dog really and truly ate his homework, she did not believe him.

Martin MacGregor had to redo his homework and miss playing kickball at recess.

Martin learned one more thing about Mrs. Payne that day: there were absolutely no excuses for no homework.

When Martin got home from school, his mother said, "I'm washing jeans, Martin. Throw in the ones you are wearing." Martin dropped his jeans into the washer and watched the water swish around the clothes, then headed upstairs to start his homework. Sadie followed close behind, hoping for more peanut butter. Martin MacGregor reached into his pocket for his spelling paper.

"My homework!" yelled Martin as he raced back downstairs to the washer. It was too late! The spin cycle had begun and Martin MacGregor's homework was faded beyond recognition.

Martin MacGregor learned on Wednesday that Mrs. Payne didn't like stiff and bleached-out homework. He had to miss kickball again and write over and over: *I will do my homework neatly. I will do my homework neatly.*

"Mr. Elliott would never make me do this," Martin mumbled under his breath.

Thursday morning was a little crazy in the MacGregor house. It was the first day of preschool for Martin's little sister. She was so excited that she practically bounced right out of her chair and didn't touch her eggs. She insisted on a backpack just like her big brother's.

His mom dropped off Martin first.
He grabbed his backpack out of the van
and raced into the room to give Mrs.
Payne his homework.

"Mrs. Payne, I have my homework today,"
Martin said excitedly. He opened his backpack.

Martin MacGregor couldn't believe his eyes.
The backpack had no homework. Instead, he
saw the yellow hair of Miss Nettie, his
sister's favorite doll.

"Looky, looky, Martin brought his dolly," cried Samuel Hall.
He grabbed Miss Nettie and started to throw her around.

Martin MacGregor tried desperately to catch Miss Nettie,
but he was unsuccessful.

Mrs. Payne was successful. She grabbed Miss Nettie in
midair and marched Martin and Samuel to the principal's office.

Martin MacGregor missed recess again. Worst of all, he had to sit next to Samuel Hall, the taker of everyone's dessert, at lunch for the rest of the week.

That evening, Martin's dad stopped by his room. "How's the homework going, son?"

Martin sighed and plopped his head down on the dictionary. "Why can't she give us something interesting for homework? This is boring."

"After you finish, why not think up your own homework?" his dad said. "What do you want to learn about? You can research it on the computer."

Martin got a fabulous idea. He spent
the rest of the evening on *his* homework.
Harriett made the perfect subject. Martin
made a book of tarantula facts. He filled his
wall with pictures of tarantulas. He made a
tarantula out of clay and pipe cleaners.

Martin even turned Sadie into a tarantula by adding extra legs to
her with his dad's black socks. At dinner, he even made one out of
his chicken and noodles.

Friday morning, Martin wasn't taking any chances. He held his stack of definitions all the way to school. As he approached the building, a sudden gust of wind sent the papers flying. No matter how fast Martin ran, the papers blew faster. He caught one, then another, but the last two did loopy loops in the sky before landing on the roof of the school.

Martin MacGregor had to redo the two lost pages of definitions, and he had to look up ten extra words. He learned homework on the roof didn't count, according to Mrs. Payne.

The next week, Martin MacGregor dragged himself into the classroom. He had put his homework carefully in his backpack, but he worried something would go wrong and Mrs. Payne would be unhappy with him.

When he got to the classroom, he couldn't believe his eyes. There was Mr. Elliott's pet tarantula, Harriett!

Martin MacGregor saw a smiling Mr. Elliott.
"Good to be back. How did last week go,
Martin?" asked Mr. Elliott.
Martin MacGregor was speechless.

At the end of the day, Mr. Elliott said,
"Class, I have your homework assignment."
The room was filled with groans.

Mr. Elliott continued, "I want you to find out everything you can about tarantulas. Whoever finds the most facts can feed Harriett next week and keep her for the weekend." The room was filled with cheers.

Martin MacGregor grinned and thought, *I wonder how my mom and sister will feel about a weekend guest?*